Amazing Grace!

How to Play Gospel Music
Book 2

Robert L. Jefferson

authorHOUSE

AuthorHouse™
1663 Liberty Drive, Suite 200
Bloomington, IN 47403
www.authorhouse.com
Phone: 1-800-839-8640

First published by AuthorHouse 2/26/2008
Second Edition; First edition copyright©2003 by Robert L. Jefferson

ISBN: 1-4208-3676-5 (sc)

Printed in the United States of America
Bloomington, Indiana

This book is printed on acid-free paper.

Fourth Edition

For information address:
Pensacola Publications, Inc., 8108 W. Osborn Rd.
Phoenix, Arizona 85033.

First Printing
Edited by Pensacola H. Jefferson

First edition entitled, Set Your Soul Free! How to play Soul Gospel, Book II.
Copyright © 1990 by Robert L. Jefferson.

 **Pensacola Publications, Inc.**
8108 W. Osborn Road•Phoenix, Arizona 85033

And God is able to make all grace abound toward you;

that ye,

always having all sufficiency in all things,

may abound to every good work:

2 Corinthians 9:8

ACKNOWLEDGMENTS

SPECIAL THANKS

-Thanks Honey, for being the special lady that you are.

-Thanks Mom and Dad, for your encouragement and support through the years.

-Thank you Lord, for your grace, understanding, and forgiveness, and for loving me just because you wanted to.

TABLE OF CONTENTS

PREFACE

After much thought and reluctance, I decided to go ahead and write book 2. There are a couple of reasons as to why I was hesitant in writing this book. First, as anyone who knows me personally can testify, I deplore writing out music note by note by note. I thank God for the invention of computer software that is able to produce music notation. Unfortunately, for the first printing of this book, I did not have a computer *nor* software available for the writing of this book. So I put it off for a while. (I never knew there were so many notes in gospel music!) Secondly, my hesitancy came from this point; I feel that one of the major problems with many musicians is their addiction to the written score. Many musicians don't trust their ear or their natural aural instincts because they have been so accustomed to reading from the written page. Believe me, I know the feeling. One of my major problems in learning jazz was weaning myself of the music and learning to trust my ear. After a while I began to notice that I would place a chord chart in front of me but would only glance at the page (it was only there for security). I felt that writing the songs and hymns out note for note would only promote the continual use of the written page instead of allowing you to depend on your natural listening abilities. But after the completion of the arrangements in book 2, I began to see how the two books fit together like hand in glove. The theoretical aspects of book 1 became more practical because book 2 enabled the student to see *and* play a song in the black gospel style without having to analyze it. Although the songs written in book 2 can stand on their own as written, I would still like to encourage you to develop your own improvisational skills and use these examples as guides to lead you into the world of soul gospel music. May God continue to increase your talents.

INTRODUCTION

People have asked, "What exactly is Soul Gospel?" My response is, "You know, Gospel, Black Gospel." As was mentioned in book one, the original term was "gospel song" or simply "gospel" and Thomas A. Dorsey, the father of gospel music, is credited with being the first person to use this term. The term "Black Gospel" is also applied to songs played in the gospel style. However, Dorsey did not enjoy using this term for the reason that gospel music is for all races and nationalities. The term "Soul Gospel" is a relatively new term in relation to gospel music. This term has been applied for clarification purposes, considering that now there are so many varied gospel styles. Therefore, the term "Gospel," "Black Gospel," and "Soul Gospel" are used synonymously. Both books demonstrate varied styles of African-American religious music, from spirituals, to hymns, to shout songs, to gospel. All of these types of songs have been placed under the general term "gospel," because of the style of piano accompaniment that is used. I hope this explanation clarifies the term "Soul Gospel."

OH, HOW I LOVE JESUS

Compare with the original hymn:

A. Triplet Subdivision: Book 1 - Chapter 8

Although the hymn was originally written in $\frac{6}{8}$ time and is also played in $\frac{6}{8}$ time in the gospel style, notice the notes marked ♪. This further subdivides the beat. The gospel arrangement is usually played a bit slower than the original hymn. The slower tempo gives the song a more laid-back, bluesy feel.

B. Passing Chords: Book 1 - Chapter 4
C. Chord Substitutions: Book 1 - Chapter 2
D. Chord Functions: Book 1 - Chapter 3

Notice measures 6, 14, and 16; a vi chord has been substituted for the original I chord. Also in measure 13; a III chord has been substituted for the I chord.

E. Secondary Dominants: Book 1 - Chapter 5

Measures 13-14 demonstrate a III to vi progression followed by I^7 to IV in measures 14-15.

F. Augmented Chords: Book 1 - Chapter 6

In measures 17 and 18 you have I^+ to vi.

G. Pentatonic Scale: Book 1 - Chapter 7

A major pentatonic scale is used in measure 10 as a lead-in to measure 11.

H. Bass Note Fills: Book 1 - Chapter 9 (e.g. 79)

Example 79 may be used in place of the bass line in measure 9-14.

I. Primary Chord Progression (Ab Major): Book 1 - Chapter 15

Oh, How I Love Jesus

Oh, How I Love Jesus

Arr. by Robert L. Jefferson

There is a name I love to hear, I love to sing its worth; It sounds like music in mine ear, the sweet - est name on earth.

me,   be - cause - - He first loved me!

PASS ME NOT

Compare with the original hymn.

      A. Passing Chords: The Book 1 - Chapter 4

      B. Triplet subdivision: Book 1 - Chapter 8

The hymn was originally written in $\frac{4}{4}$ time but it is traditionally sung in $\frac{12}{8}$ time.

      C. Major Pentatonic Scale: Book 1 - Chapter 7

In measure 8, a major pentatonic scale is used to lead into measure 9, also in measure 12 leading to measure 13 and other places throughout.

      D. Major Scale: Book 1 - Chapter 7

Measure 16 (ending).

      E. Bass Line Movement: Book 1 - Chapter 9 (e.g. 80)

      F. Waterfalls: Book 1 - Chapter 10

Measure 5 and other measures throughout. Chordal arpeggios are also used as in measure 16.

      G. Chord Substitutions: Book 1 - Chapter 2

      H. Chord Functions: Book 1 - Chapter 3

In measure 6, vi is used in place of the original I chord. In measure 11, $\frac{vii\o^7}{V}$ is used in place of I.

      I. Secondary Dominants: Book 1 - Chapter 5

In measure 6, III^7 to vi, in measure 11-12, $\frac{vii\o^7}{V}$ to V^7.

      J. Turns: Book 1 - Chapter 10 (e.g. 87a-d)

In measure 4, turns are played in octaves.

      K. Chromaticism: Book 1 - Chapter 7 (e.g. 63a & b)

In measure 4, chromaticism is used in conjunction with turns in the same measure.

      L. Primary Chord Progression (Ab Major): Book 1 - Chapter 15

Pass Me Not

Pass Me Not

Arr. by Robert L. Jefferson

* E against Eb causes tension but quickly resolves

do - not pass me by.

AMAZING GRACE

The hymn *"Amazing Grace"* is a standard hymn in black churches and is commonly called the "Hymn of the Church." It is traditionally sung prior to or following the sermon. This example was written in free meter and transitions into $\frac{9}{8}$ meter. However, when played for a congregation it will either be played in free meter *or* $\frac{9}{8}$ time, but not both. In more traditional Baptist church services it is most commonly sung in free meter, either with or without instrumental accompaniment. Compare the gospel arrangement to the original hymn.

A. Free Meter: Book 1 - Chapter 12

B. Triplet Subdivision: Book 1 - Chapter 8 (e.g. 67 & 68)

C. Chromatic Scale: Book 1 - Chapter 7 (e.g. 63a & b)

D. Minor Pentatonic Scale: Book 1 - Chapter 7 (e.g. 62a & b)
Measure 8, played in octaves.

E. Arpeggios: Book 1 - Chapter 7 (e.g. 66)
Measure 4. double handed arpeggio.

F. Pedal Tones: book 1 - Chapter 11 (e.g. 95)
Measures 14 and 15, $\frac{9}{8}$ section.

G. Inversions: Book 1 - Chapter 10 (e.g. 90 & 91)

H. Grace Note and Blues Gospel Licks: Book 1 - Chapter 10 (e.g. 96a)
Measure 26.

I. Waterfalls: book 1 - Chapter 10 (e.g. 85)
Used throughout.

J. Chord Substitutions: Book 1 - Chapter 2

K. Chord Functions: Book 1 - Chapter 3
In measure 20 and 21, a vi to $\frac{vii\varnothing^7}{V}$ is used instead of the original I chords in measure 5 and 6 of the original hymn.

L. Suspensions: Book 1 - Chapter 10 (e.g. 92a)
Measure 22, resolving to the dominant in measure 23.

M. Primary Chord Progression (Ab Major): Book 1 - Chapter 15

Amazing Grace

AMAZING GRACE

Free meter - follow vocalist unless played as a piano solo
Voice - Ad lib

Arr. by Robert L. Jefferson

12

that — saved ... a — wretch ... like — me! — ... I — once

* Dissonance is common.

found,

was blind

but now

sweet — the — sound; — That —

saved a wretch — like —

me!

** The vocal triplet figures should be laid back, not rushed.

JUST A CLOSER WALK WITH THEE

"*Just a Closer Walk with Thee*" is traditionally sung as a solo or solo with choir rather than as a congregational song. This arrangement was written in free meter. Unlike "*Amazing Grace*," which is sung in free *or* in $\frac{12}{8}$ time, "*Just a Closer Walk with Thee*" may either be sung in free meter, in $\frac{12}{8}$ time, or in free meter with a transition into $\frac{12}{8}$ time. Compare the gospel arrangement with the original song.

     A. Free Meter: Book 1 - Chapter 12

     B. Triplet Subdivision: Book 1 - Chapter 8

     C. Altered Chords: Book 1 - Chapter 6 (e.g. 56)

     D. Chromaticism: Book 1 - Chapter 11 (e.g. 98)
Measures 24 through 25.

     E. Arpeggios: Book 1 - Chapter 7 (e.g. 65)
Measure 20, descending into measure 21.

     F. Chromatic Passing Chords: Book 1 - Chapter 4 (e.g. 33b)
Throughout.

     G. Suspensions: Book 1 - Chapter 10 (e.g. 92b)
Measure 3, leading to I^7.

     H. Bass Line Movement: Book 1 - Chapter 9 (e.g. 80)
Measure 22.

Just A Closer Walk With Thee

Just a clo - ser walk with Thee,

Grant it Je - sus if you please,

Dai - ly walk - ing close to Thee,

Let it be dear Lord, let it be.

Just A Closer Walk With Thee

free meter

Arr. by Robert L. Jefferson

JESUS

"*Jesus*" is a blues gospel choral arrangement written in the traditional gospel style. This piece demonstrates the walking bass line as well as the "blue" notes, which are necessary to obtain a "gritty" blues sound. Also notice the use of the solo lead vocal lines. The use of a lead vocalist is a standard practice in black gospel music. Also notice that the lead vocalist has the freedom to ad lib throughout. The written manuscript is merely a guide as to how the song should be performed.

     A. Triplet Subdivision: Book 1 - chapter 8

     B. Walking Bass Line: Book 1 - Chapter 9 (e.g. 81a & b)

     C. Blues Gospel Fills: Book 1 - Chapter 11 (e.g. 96a & b)
Measure 19.

     D. Blues Scale: Book 1 - Chapter 10 (e.g. 86a)

     E. Minor Pentatonic Scale: Book 1 - Chapter 10 (e.g. 86b)

JESUS

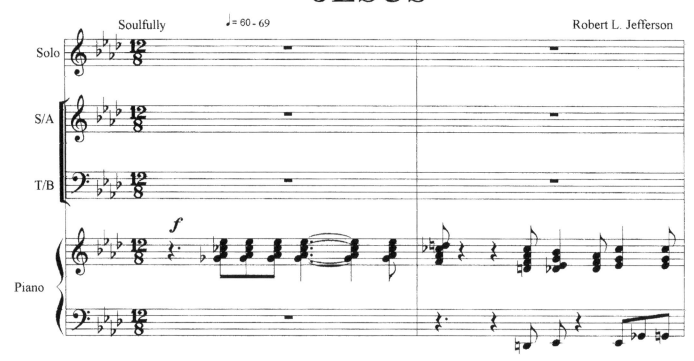

One of these days,   I want to see His
One of these days,   Oo,   Ooh,   I want to see His

face.   1.   2.
face.   Oo, Ooh,   Oo, Ooh.   Ooh.

I WOKE UP THIS MORNING

"I Woke Up This Morning with My Mind Stayed on Jesus" is a spiritual that is traditionally sung as a congregational song in many black churches. Several spirituals were taken from the south and later adapted into gospel songs. This song has a shuffle type of feel and should not be played too fast or too slow. Look for the following elements:

A. Chord Repetition: Book 1 - Chapter 10 (e.g. 84)

B. Major Pentatonic Scale: Book 1 - Chapter 7 (e.g. 61b)
Measure 15, leading into measure 16.

I WOKE UP THIS MORNING

Traditional

Arr. by Robert L. Jefferson

* If singing more than one verse, play the 2nd ending only and repeat the next verse.

SING HIM A NEW SONG

"Sing Him A New Song" was written in the traditional gospel style. The traditional gospel style is very blues oriented. Other songs in this style are, *"Too Close to Heaven,"* by Alex Bradford and *"Another Days Journey,"* by Inez Andrews.

A. Triplet Subdivision: Book 1 - Chapter 8
"Sing Him A New Song" demonstrates triplet subdivision in $\frac{9}{8}$ time instead of $\frac{12}{8}$ time.

B. Gospel Fills: Book 1 - Chapter 11 (e.g. 97)
Measure 1.

C. Chord Repetition: Book 1 - Chapter 10
Repetition between the I and ii chords in measure 6 and repetition from IV^7 to I in measure 20 and 21, also other measures throughout.

D. Glissando: Book 1 - Chapter 10
Ascending white key glissando in measure 11.

E. Bass Line: parallel, contrary, and oblique motion Book 1 - Chapter 9
Parallel motion in measure 3-4, contrary motion in measure 24-25, and oblique motion in measure 9-10.

F. Altered Chords: Book 1 - Chapter 6 (e.g. 54a & b)
In measure 11-13 you have ii^7 - $\frac{viio^7}{V}$ - $I\frac{6}{4}$ (pedal D as the dominant) $\frac{viio}{vi}$ - vi^7.

G. Secondary Dominants: Book 1 - Chapter 5 (e.g. 39-40)
Measures 23-24, III^7 to vi.

H. Passing Chords: Book 1 - Chapter 4 (e.g. 33c)
Measure 26.

I. Waterfalls: Book 1 - Chapter 10
Throughout.

J. Scale Lead-ins: Book 1 - Chapter 7 (e.g. 59b)
Measure 27, leading into measure 28.

K. Arpeggios: Book 1 - Chapter 7 (e.g. 66)
Ascending double handed arpeggio in measure 28.

SING HIM A NEW SONG

The 16th notes should be played with a ♪♪ feel.

Robert L. Jefferson

* The 16th notes in this measure should be played staight.
** 8va on repeat only

* Repeat and ad lib as many times as desired.

** The 16th notes in this measure should be played straight.

CALVARY

"Calvary," like several other African-American melodies, is written in a minor key which stresses the mournful theme of the song. This song is usually performed by a choir or soloist and on occasion, as a congregational hymn. This song is unique in that a melodic minor scale is used rather than a natural or harmonic minor scale. Notice that in measure 5 and 6, the ascending melodic line uses a B♮ and not a B♭. In measure 7-8, the descending melodic line uses a B♭. The C melodic minor scale is made up of the following notes and intervals:

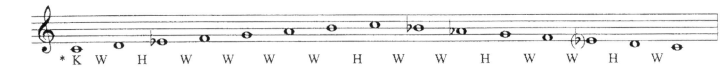

Also notice:

     A. Minor Subdominant: Book 1 - Chapter 2 (e.g. 19a-c) Measures 20-21.

     B. Triplet Feel Throughout: Book 1 - Chapter 8

     C. Double Handed Arpeggio: Book 1 – Chapter 7 (e.g. 66) Measure 16.

     * K = key note
       W = whole step
       H = half step

CALVARY

CALVARY

Arr. by Robert L. Jefferson

Cal - va - ry, Cal va - ry, sure - ly He - died on Cal - va - ry.

ENTER HIS COURTS WITH PRAISE

"Enter His Courts with Praise" was written to demonstrate a song in strict forward drive. These types of gospel songs are often performed by a choir along with instrumental accompaniment. Pay particular attention to the driving octave bass line.

     A. Strict Forward Drive: Book 1 - chapter 8 (e.g. 69)

     B. Bass Line Movement: Book 1 - Chapter 8 (e.g. 71)

     C. Syncopation: Book 1 - Chapter 8

     D. Duple Meter: (3 against 2)
Measures 14-17.

ENTER HIS COURTS WITH PRAISE

Robert L. Jefferson

* Repeat B as many times as desired.

43

14

17   DC al Coda

GUIDE ME, O' THOU GREAT JEHOVAH

It is common to sing *"Guide Me, O' Thou Great Jehovah"* in both the original hymn form and in free meter. The free metered or long metered version is an example of call and response, where one person chants a section of a song and the congregation enters afterwards. These types of songs were originally sung a cappella, but now that instruments are common place in the worship service, they are often accompanied by piano and/or organ. Free metered songs are not always performed by the congregation. It is also common for soloists to sing songs or hymns in free meter, such as the song, *"Precious Lord, Take My Hand,"* by Thomas A. Dorsey.

A. Free Meter: Book 1 - Chapter 12

Moments of silence should be avoided and used only for special effects. This is the purpose for using left hand tremolo.

Guide Me, O' Thou Great Jehovah

Guide me, O' Thou great Je - ho - vah, Pil - grim

through this bar - ren land. I am weak but Thou art

migh - ty; hold me with Thy pow'r - ful hand. Bread of

Hea - ven feed me 'till I want no - more, Bread of

Hea - ven feed me 'till I want no more.

GUIDE ME, O' THOU GREAT JEHOVAH

Free meter   Traditional   Arr. by Robert L. Jefferson

- I am weak, but Thou art mighty; Hold me with Thy powerful hand;
- Bread of Heaven, bread of Heaven, feed me 'till I want no more.

Pil - - - - - grim - through this bar - - - ren - - land;

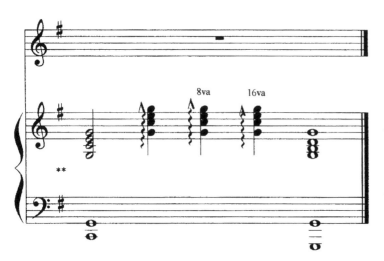

8va   16va

* ⌣ is a symbol denoting scoops or bends into the pitch. This is done to stress a particular word or add intensity to the meaning of the text.

** This is an optional ending which may be played at the completion of the final verse.

RUNNING FOR MY LORD

"Running for My Lord" demonstrates another form of call and response where one person in the congregation sings a line of a song and the congregation enters with the answer or response. This type of call and response is much faster than free-metered call and response songs. Songs of this type are commonly heard in black holiness churches, where they are accompanied by percussion, clapping, dancing and shouting. Pay particular attention to the duple metered sections. This song is marked $\downarrow$ equals 144-152. Sometimes shout songs of this type are played even faster. Look for the following:

A. Bass Line Movement: Book 1 - Chapter 9 (e.g. 82 & 83)

B. Blues Scale: Book 1 - Chapter 10 (e.g. 86a)

C. Duple Meter: (3 against 2)
Measures 32-34.

D. Syncopation: Book 1 - Chapter 8
Throughout.

E. Cadences: Book 1 - Chapter 2
*In measures 16-17 a plagal cadence may also be used. The IV-I cadence is very common at the end of shout songs, even more common than the V-I cadence.

RUNNING FOR MY LORD

Robert L. Jefferson

2. L: I'm on my way to Heaven,   C: Can't turn back...

C: Can't turn back, T: Yes, I'm run - nin' for my

Lord, and I can't turn back!

* This bass line may also be used for measures 32 - 34.
** Repeat as many times as desired.

MAKE MY LIFE A LIVING SACRIFICE

"Make My Life a Living Sacrifice" is a choral arrangement that demonstrates a strong 2nd & 4th beat. It has a very laid back feel and uses syncopation to the fullest. When you hear a song in this style, you immediately say, "That's Gospel!"

Look for the following elements:

A. Syncopation: Book 1 - Chapter 8 (e.g. 70)
Measure 8 and throughout.

B. Bass Line and Inversions: Book 1 - Chapter 9 (e.g. 74a & b)
Measure 10 and throughout.

C. Chromaticism: Book 1 - Chapter 14
Measure 17 and throughout letter B.

D. Glissando: Book 1 - Chapter 10
Black key glissandos, measure 27.

MAKE MY LIFE A LIVING SACRIFICE

Words by Robert L. and Pensacola H. Jefferson

Robert L. Jefferson

mf Lord, make my life a liv-ing sac - ri - fice, Lord, let no- one see me,

just Je - sus Christ; Lord, I de - di - cate my life to you,

* Bass line may be omitted. Gospel is commonly sung in three part harmony.

Help me lift you up, for all the world to see Your glo - ry,

Help me praise Your name, for You a - lone are wor - thy,

Help me live my life ho - ly com - mit - ted un - to

* Chorus clap on beats 2 and 4 during a cappella section.

lost and all a - lone. Oh, but Je - sus took me in. He

gave me peace with - in, no lon - ger shall I roam, for Your

love has brought me home. Your love, Your love, has lif - ted me,

Your love, Your love, Your love has lif - ted me,

* 2nd X, instruments re-enter

58

DC al Coda

DC al Coda

* Repeat to B: Chorus a cappella until measure 24.

MEDITATION AND PRAISE

The contemporary soul gospel sound is produced by an extensive use of 9th, 11th, and 13th chords. These chords are meshed together by the use of chromatic passing chords and chord substitutions. Read chapter 14 in book one to become more familiar with the contemporary soul gospel style.

    A. Chromaticism: Book 1 - Chapter 14 (e.g. 106a & 108)
Measure 9 and (example 104) measure 6-7.

    B. Syncopation: Book 1 - Chapter 8
Used throughout.

MEDITATION AND PRAISE

Do not play the 16th notes too straight.

Robert L. Jefferson

decresc

DC al Coda *

* Repeat to either letter B or to letter A and take Coda

WHAT A FRIEND WE HAVE IN JESUS

This arrangement demonstrates the extensive use of suspensions, chord substitutions, and chromaticism. Compare with the original hymn.

A. Suspensions: Book 1 - Chapter 10 (e.g. 92a & b)
    Book 1 - Chapter 11 (e.g. 93-94a-c)
Suspensions are used throughout.

B. Chord Substitutions: Book 1 - Chapter 2 (e.g. 15 & 16)
$ii^{\o7}$ substituted for IV in measures 2 and 16, and throughout.

C. Chromaticism: Book 1 - Chapter 14
Used throughout.

D. Primary Chord Progression: Book 1 - Chapter 15

WHAT A FRIEND WE HAVE IN JESUS

WHAT A FRIEND WE HAVE IN JESUS

Arr. by Robert L. Jefferson

AMAZING GRACE

This is a relatively conservative contemporary arrangement of *"Amazing Grace."* It includes tritone substitutions, suspensions, chromaticism, chord substitutions, and the extensive use of 9th, 11th and 13th chords. Although this and other more elaborate arrangements are very pleasing to hear, be careful about playing hymns too elaborately when accompanying a congregation. I can recall worship services where the hymns were so embellished with contemporary harmonies that they were unrecognizable and the congregation had great difficulty following. As always, use your creativity with discretion and good taste, always keeping in mind the place and the occasion.

A. Chromaticism: Book 1 - Chapter 14
Measure 3 and throughout.

B. Tritone Substitutions: Book 1 - Chapter 14 (e.g. 100c)

C. Suspensions: Book 1 - Chapter 10 (e.g. 92a)
Measure 5 and throughout.

D. Contemporary Harmonies and Altered Chords: Book 1 - chapter 14 (e.g. 100d-100c)
Throughout.

E. Chord Substitutions: Book 1 - Chapter 3
Used throughout.

AMAZING GRACE

Slowly

Arr. by Robert L. Jefferson

once – – was – lost   but   now – – I'm – –

found,   was   blind   but – – now   I

see.

POWER IN THE BLOOD

"Power in the Blood" is an old camp meeting type hymn and is marked ♩ =100. I have heard it played faster and slower. Compare this arrangement with the original hymn and look for the following musical elements:

A. Bass Line: Book 1 - Chapter 9 (e.g. 82)
Single line walking bass throughout.

B. Chord Repetition: Book 1 - Chapter 10 (e.g. 84)
Used throughout.

C. Chromaticism: Book 1 - Chapter 14 (e.g. 106a & 106b)
Measure 1 and 2 and throughout.

D. Minor Pentatonic Scale: Book 1 - Chapter 7 (e.g. 62a & b)
Measure 14.

E. Fills: Book 1 - Chapter 10 (e.g. 97)
Measure 12 and throughout.

F. Secondary Dominants: Book 1 - Chapter 5 (e.g. 41-42)
Measures 35-42.

G. Endings: Book 1 - Chapter 10 (e.g. 98)
Measures 43-44.

H. Primary Chord Progression: Book 1 - Chapter 15

Power In The Blood

POWER IN THE BLOOD

Arr. by Robert L. Jefferson

WORSHIP

"*Worship*" makes use of chord voicings that are very prevalent in contemporary gospel music. These chords may be used throughout a song as dominant functioning chords <u>or</u> as passing chords.

A.   Contemporary Harmonies: Book 1 – chapter 14 (e.g. 106a)
Measure 13.

B.   Contemporary Harmonies: Book 1 – chapter 14 (e.g. 112a)
Measure 21.

C.   Contemporary Harmonies: Book 1 – chapter 14 (e.g. 112c)
Measure 35 and 36.

D.   Contemporary Harmonies: Book 1 – chapter 14 (e.g. 112c)
Measures 42 and 43.

WORSHIP

Robert L. Jefferson

praise. You praise.

Tenors: Lord, we love You, — — mag- ni - fy Your

name. We a - dore You, — — Lord, we lift You up! **

Add Altos: Lord, we love You, — —

- mag- ni - fy Your name. We a - dore You — — Lord, we lift You up! **

35   36

* You may shorten the song by ending on beat one of measure 26.

** Each 4 bar section may be repeated as many times as desired.

* 1st Sopranos may sing the tenor part one octave higher in this section.

TRANSCRIPTIONS

Use the next few pages to transcribe gospel chords and licks that you hear or that you make up.
Or compose your own gospel song or arrangement. Be creative. Remember, 2 Corinthians 9:8.

NOTES

NOTES

312-41742   DRY BONZ!   arr. Robert L. Jefferson $2.60
S.A.T.B., a cappella
Sacred (General)

DRY BONZ!

FOR S.A.T.B. CHORUS, A CAPPELLA

SPIRITUAL
ARRANGED BY ROBERT L. JEFFERSON

From Robert L. Jefferson, comes "Dry Bonz!" (312-41742) on the Theodore Presser imprint. This is a great setting of the spiritual for SATB chorus, a cappella. Jefferson is an expert in the performance of black gospel music, and is author of the book, "How to Play Black Gospel for Beginners" and other books on how to play black gospel music. You will want to take a look at this exciting spiritual from Jefferson! To order this piece, contact your favorite print music dealer or contact Presser at 610-525-3636.

Also from Robert L. Jefferson, comes "A Pilgrim and a Stranger" (0-19-386444-4), published by Oxford University Press. To order these pieces, contact your favorite print music dealer.

You Can Play Gospel Music Now!!!
www.jeffersonpresents.com

Precious Lord! Bk 1 provides the foundation for playing Gospel Music.
INTERMEDIATE to ADVANCED
Amazing Grace! Bk 2 offers note for note arrangements and works hand in hand with Precious Lord, BK 1.

How to Play Gospel Music for Beginners will enable you to play Gospel Music *and* learn how to play the piano at the same time!
BEGINNING to INTERMEDIATE
How to Play Gospel Music for Beginners Bk 2 is a supplement to How to Play Gospel Music for Beginners. Over 70 multi-level arrangements!

Fill out the order form, detach and mail to the address below

Order Form
Pensacola Publications, PO Box 9, Avenue, MD 20609 USA. Telephone 1-800-289-9258
PLEASE SEND THE FOLLOWING BOOKS and CDs

___How to Play Gospel Music for Beginners $22.95___CD $9.95

___How to Play Gospel Music for Beginners Bk 2 $22.95___CD $9.95

___Amazing Grace! How to Play Gospel Music $22.95___CD $9.95

___Precious Lord! How to Play Gospel Music $24.95___CD $9.95

___DVD How to Play Gospel Music by Ear___ DVD $39.95
*Add $7.00 S&H for books; $3.00 S&H for CDs/DVD: $9.50 S&H for books, CDs &DVD   Total_____

NAME_____ADDRESS_____

CITY/STATE/ZIP_____
ENCLOSE CHECK OR MONEY ORDER AND MAIL TO THE ABOVE ADDRESS
Credit Cards Accepted:
{}Master Card {}Visa {}American Express {}Discover {}Divers {}JCB
Card Num & Exp Date (Include Last 3 or 4 numbers on back of Card if listed)_____

Signature_____Phone#_____
Satisfaction Guaranteed or your money back!

About the Author

Robert L. Jefferson holds a Bachelor of Science degree from Grand Canyon University, Phoenix, Arizona, a Master of Music degree from the University of Houston, and a Doctor of Musical Arts Degree from the University of Maryland. He began playing the piano for the church at the age of nine. Dr. Jefferson was able to refine his gospel style by serving as pianist for the Mount Calvary Baptist Church, the Salt River Valley District Association Congress and the Arizona National Baptist Convention. He also promoted the gospel style of piano playing through his private piano students. After leaving Phoenix, he served as organist for the Christian Fellowship of Musicians and Entertainers and taught class piano at the University of Houston. Jefferson has had extensive performing experience as pianist for a variety of gospel artists throughout the United States and Asia. While in Japan, he was musical director of the Yokota Inspirational Gospel Choir in Tokyo and also educator for numerous Japanese gospel choirs and musicians throughout Japan. He is experienced as a soloist, songwriter, recording artist and jazz pianist and continues to perform and conduct workshops nationally and internationally. It is Dr. Jefferson's desire that his books will aid in elevating the spread of gospel music education throughout the world.

Made in the USA
Las Vegas, NV
13 June 2022

50174022R00062